Not Waving

Also by Catherine Hayes

SKIRMISHES

Not Waving

Catherine Hayes

faber and faber
LONDON · BOSTON

First published in 1984
by Faber and Faber Limited
3 Queen Square London WC1N 3AU
Filmset by Wilmaset Birkenhead Merseyside
Printed in Great Britain by
Redwood Burn Limited Trowbridge Wiltshire

British Library Cataloguing in Publication Data

Hayes, Catherine
Not waving.
I. Title
822'.914   PR6058.A/

ISBN 0–571–13129–8

Library of Congress data has been applied for

Characters

JILL
HARRY
MIRIAM

The action takes place in a cabaret club.

Not Waving was first performed at the Traverse Theatre, Edinburgh on 7 October 1982.

The cast was as follows:

JILL	Carmel McSharry
HARRY	Sean Scanlon
MIRIAM	Lynne Miller
Director	Peter Lichtenfels
Designer	David Cockayne
Lighting	Colin Scott

ACT ONE

JILL *is sitting alone waiting for* HARRY*'s return from a meeting with the management. She looks preoccupied. Enter* HARRY.

JILL: Well?

HARRY: I've been as quick as I could.

JILL: Did you see Maurice?

HARRY: No.

JILL: He came to the dressing room half an hour ago.

HARRY: How did you get rid of him?

JILL: I slammed the door.

HARRY: In his face?

JILL: No, on his fingers. The tops of them are lying up there on the carpet. He went away crying.

HARRY: Ah, he's not so bad. Poor old Maurice.

JILL: Poor old Maurice. He's only my age.

HARRY: He looks older.

JILL: We'd all look older if we were cooped up in a place like this.

HARRY: It's all right.

JILL: Oh, Harry, where's your taste? It's a dump.

HARRY: It's OK.

JILL: It's not the best place I ever played in.

HARRY: No, and it's not the worst.

JILL: You wouldn't know about the worst. It was before your time.

HARRY: Who was your manager then?

JILL: I don't know. I can't remember. I went through them quicker in those days.

HARRY: Maybe that was your mistake. You should've stuck
to one.
JILL: I tried but he kept sliding off.
(*Short pause.*)
JILL: He was looking for you actually.
HARRY: Maurice?
JILL: Yes.
HARRY: What for?
JILL: You know.
HARRY: What did you say?
JILL: I said, 'On no account.'
HARRY: It's only what he's entitled to.
JILL: He hasn't given me what I'm entitled to.
HARRY: He's doing his best.
JILL: I can't stand the man.
HARRY: That's got nothing to do with it.
JILL: I don't have to work with people I don't like.
HARRY: You do.
(*Short pause.*)
JILL: (*Sighs*) Well, if you want to arrange something, fair
enough, but I'm not having him pestering me.
HARRY: He doesn't pester anyone. He begs for an audience.
JILL: Well, tell him to come here in an hour. We can run it
through again then.
(*Short pause.*)
HARRY: The management wants more than a run-through.
JILL: What d'ye mean?
HARRY: They want some changes.
JILL: They can want.
HARRY: They're serious.
JILL: I don't care if they're terminal, I'm not changing
anything for their benefit.
HARRY: I think you should consider it.
JILL: Thanks for the advice.
HARRY: Jill, you've got nothing to lose. What harm can it do

on your last night?

JILL: What would be the point? They booked me. If they don't like me now, that's their hard luck. I'm not so keen on them.

HARRY: Last night wasn't all that good, was it?

JILL: It's a free country. People don't have to laugh.

HARRY: You've got to have an eye to the future. They were thinking of asking you back.

JILL: Were they?

HARRY: Yes.

JILL: Was that your idea?

HARRY: I suggested it and they were agreeable.

JILL: But they're not so agreeable now?

HARRY: No.

JILL: Good enough.

HARRY: It's not good enough.

JILL: Harry, it's just one theatre club. Who cares?

HARRY: Things get around.

JILL: What things?

HARRY: Well, they won't blame Maurice, will they?

JILL: I don't know what they'll do. They're not my kind of people.

HARRY: Everything's in a bit of a mess, that's all.

JILL: Harry, you're business, I'm entertainment. You're management, I'm audience. Let's keep it that way.

HARRY: You're not making things easy.

JILL: I pay you to sort out the problems. If I could sort them out myself I'd save a lot of money. You should be grateful to me for being inadequate.

HARRY: This isn't my problem.

JILL: Shut it.

HARRY: If that's all you can say.

JILL: It's not all I can say, but it's all I'm going to say.
    (*Pause.*)

HARRY: You'll have to do something about the songs at least.

11

JILL: The songs are fine.

HARRY: Well, could you synchronize them with the music?

JILL: Maurice plays everything in 3/4 time.

HARRY: Sing in 3/4 time then.

JILL: (*Deliberately patronizing*) I'll try.

HARRY: That wasn't too painful, was it?

JILL: No, it was very nice. I'm a good girl.

HARRY: Yes, you are . . . And you'll have to get together with Maurice in about twenty minutes.

JILL: Why?

HARRY: Because that fits in with his schedule.

JILL: Would you like me to tell him what to do with his schedule?

HARRY: No.

JILL: What a shame.

(*Pause.*)

HARRY: You know the way these people are, Jill. They tend to worry.

JILL: They're not going to go bankrupt because of me.

HARRY: No.

JILL: Well, what's the fuss for, then?

HARRY: It's just one of those things. They get edgy.

JILL: They want to try telling jokes every night. They'd soon find out what edgy is. The toilet paper I go through.

HARRY: Oh yes, and that's another thing. They asked could you please not hog the facilities?

JILL: What facilities?

HARRY: Well, you were there a long time last night.

JILL: Have they only got the one?

HARRY: There's the dancers to cater for, too.

JILL: Dancers can do it anywhere. I know, I used to be one.

HARRY: Well nowadays they go for personal hygiene, feminine deodorants, that kind of thing. It's considered very attractive.

JILL: Is it? Well, tell them to stick a bunch of flowers there.

12

It'd improve the look of the thing if nothing else.

HARRY: Could you just go at regular intervals tonight, please, and not immediately before any other act is due on stage?

JILL: I'll run round to the bus station if you like.

HARRY: Whatever you think is best.

(*Short pause.*)

JILL: Previous managers of mine wouldn't've stood for this, you know.

HARRY: What would they've stood for?

JILL: They'd've made sure I was treated like a star. I'm the name that's providing these others with an audience.

HARRY: They've still got to go to the toilet.

JILL: Oh, the place is a dump. What did we come here for?

(*Pause.*)

HARRY: They want to know if you're putting something new in.

JILL: It's not that easy to come up with new material.

HARRY: You could try some out.

JILL: If I had any.

HARRY: You can think of something. A few gags. One-liners.

JILL: D'you think it's easier to write a one-liner than a two-liner?

HARRY: I doubt if it's that easy to write any.

JILL: Well, why d'ye suggest I do it now, then? I can't just sit down and write jokes. It's not like knitting a pair of socks.

HARRY: You can't do that either.

JILL: You're getting on my nerves.

HARRY: It was only a joke.

(*Short pause.*)

JILL: Has Miriam been in touch?

HARRY: No.

JILL: Or David?

HARRY: Not that I know of.

13

JILL: You mean he might've been?

HARRY: It's possible.

JILL: Was there anything for me in the rack?

HARRY: No.

JILL: What about at the hotel? I left before the second post.

HARRY: There was nothing.

JILL: They're both illiterate anyway.

HARRY: (*Lightly*) They'll be in touch when they want something.

JILL: I know.

(*Short pause.*)

HARRY: There are worse places than this.

JILL: Take no notice of me, Harry.

HARRY: I wouldn't've booked it for you if it wasn't OK. I came here first. I checked everything. I made inquiries.

JILL: It's fine.

HARRY: This should've been a great week.

JILL: It is a great week.

(*Short pause.*)

HARRY: D'ye want me to give Miriam a ring?

JILL: No.

HARRY: What abou—

JILL: (*Interrupting*) He's not on the phone. He used to be but he had it taken out. Along with a few other things.

HARRY: It's no good sitting here hoping they'll come. If you want them . . .

JILL: I don't want them. I never wanted them. Biggest mistake of my life.

HARRY: Yes. Well, we all make mistakes.

JILL: What's that supposed to mean?

HARRY: Nothing. Something to say, that's all.

JILL: If we've reached the stage of filling up the space between us with conversational niceties, it really is time for a change.

HARRY: It's not time for a change. Don't read deep

significance into every remark I make.

JILL: No, but if I bore you that much . . .

HARRY: I never said you bored me.

JILL: You left me with that impression.

HARRY: Maybe it's the wrong impression.

JILL: I'm good at assessing the mood of an audience.

HARRY: I'm not an audience.

JILL: (*Trying to explain*) Look, I know . . . Oh, never mind.

HARRY: I wish you wouldn't worry so much. You're still a very attractive woman.

JILL: Still.

HARRY: Well, if you're going to be sensitive.

JILL: D'ye really think I'm worried about the way I look? This face has been staring out of mirrors for years. I wish I could see what *it* sees.

HARRY: Are you still on those tablets?

JILL: Oh, thanks, Harry. I thought I'd made a statement of some substance there. I was trying to formulate a great truth.

HARRY: Are you taking the tablets or aren't you?

JILL: (*Irritated*) Which ones?

HARRY: I don't know which ones.

JILL: You've slept four foot six inches away from them every night for the last two months.

HARRY: Except this week.

JILL: Except this week.
    (*Short pause.*)

HARRY: Are you taking them?

JILL: Have you noticed any change in me? Any improvement or any deterioration?

HARRY: (*After a long pause*) No.

JILL: Well, then.
    (*Short pause.*)

HARRY: I've had a lot on my mind just recently.

JILL: You wouldn't notice if I'd had my teeth out and a set of kitchen units put in.

HARRY: I would.

JILL: Well, for your information I am taking the tablets. I have been taking them non-stop since the doctor prescribed them for me. I don't know what effect they're supposed to have. He didn't say. I don't know whether my feet turn blue, or my navel sprouts cauliflower. I don't know whether to expect my toenails to tickle my ear lobes, or what. But I am taking the tablets. For better, for worse. For richer, for poorer. In sickness and in health, I am taking the tablets. I'm dosing myself to buggery. Does that answer your question?

HARRY: Yes.

JILL: Well, don't bring the subject up again!

HARRY: I won't.

(*Pause.*)

JILL: (*Still angry*) I've never taken tablets before in my life.

HARRY: You must've done.

JILL: I haven't.

HARRY: Everybody takes tablets at some time or other.

JILL: I don't.

HARRY: They do you no harm.

JILL: I don't know what they're for!

HARRY: They're to calm you down.

JILL: (*Shouting*) I am calm!

(*Pause.*)

JILL: At least I was calm before I started taking them. I think he gave me the wrong ones. These must be for you.

HARRY: Oh, knock it off.

JILL: God, I'd like to smash Maurice over the head. Did you hear that cacophony last night?

HARRY: It wasn't so bad.

JILL: Whose manager are you?

HARRY: Jill, there were quite a few things wrong with last night's show.

16

JILL: (*On the defensive*) Really?

HARRY: Yes.

JILL: With the whole show?

HARRY: Yes.

JILL: Tell me.

HARRY: The singer had a bad throat.

JILL: That improved him.

HARRY: The dancers have fat legs.

JILL: They've had them all week.

HARRY: It's very difficult to lust after heavy thighs. All the men in the audience were disappointed . . . And you weren't on top form, were you?

JILL: No.

HARRY: So you can't blame Maurice entirely.

JILL: It's very difficult for a comedian to be on top form every night.

HARRY: I know it is.

JILL: No one's on top form every night. Not night after night. Not every single night. None of us is that good.

HARRY: No.

JILL: I've been doing my best, Harry. It wasn't deliberate.

HARRY: You were good, Jill. You were very good . . . But it wasn't your best.

JILL: Why not?

HARRY: You kept missing the mark. You timed it badly. It's as you say: some nights are better than others.

JILL: That's true. It really is. Why worry?

HARRY: Tonight'll be great.

JILL: Yeah, it will. I think you're right. I've had my little tantrum . . . (*Much calmer now*) Was there anything in particular they wanted me to go over?

HARRY: The first song. They're not keen on it.

JILL: Oh, I like that.

JILL: (*She sings with gusto:*)
    Send for the midwife, Mary,

17

> Something in my belly's gone pop.
> Ta-ra. Ta-ra-ra-ra-ra-r-a-ra.

HARRY: They think it's old-fashioned.

JILL: It is.

HARRY: They want something more up to date.

JILL: (*Not sadly*) They don't want me, then, do they?

HARRY: Don't be like that.

JILL: No one loves a fairy when she's forty. Or fifty. Or more. And God help her if she can't get her arse into a size 38 any longer. It's a fate worse than death.

HARRY: It must be years since you were in a size 38.

JILL: It's about nine managers ago.

HARRY: Listen, Jill, give them what they want. Keep them at bay. It's only one more night. Drop the song.

JILL: OK. It's dropped. As the woman said with the prolapse.

HARRY: Good. I feel better now.

JILL: I'm glad someone does.

HARRY: It is only one song.

JILL: You mean they find the other songs acceptable? Foot-tapping?

HARRY: More or less. Don't worry about them. It was that one in particular they didn't like. And you must admit the audience didn't laugh.

JILL: They couldn't hear the words. Maurice was playing the 1812 Overture.

HARRY: Well anyway, as long as we've got it sorted out . . . Oh, and don't do any ethnic jokes. They're trying to change the image of this place. They want to attract a different class of customer.

JILL: I should imagine the building's proximity to the gas works would go some way towards dictating the type of clientele they can expect.

HARRY: That's where you're wrong. It's only just off the motorway. It's accessible to thousands.

JILL: They're not coming, though, are they?

HARRY: The management reckons they haven't found the right type of show yet.

JILL: What they really mean is that I'm chasing away their customers.

HARRY: They didn't say that.

JILL: They've no need to. I've met these people before. They don't bother me. I don't blame my failure on someone else.

HARRY: Only Maurice.

JILL: I deserve that. I accept it. Gracefully . . . It's not Maurice's fault that I'm going through a bad patch.

HARRY: You're not going through a bad patch. Not as far as your career's concerned.

JILL: Wherever I go these days, there always seems to be a Maurice.

HARRY: You haven't had as many laughs this week, that's all.

JILL: It's not all.

HARRY: It's what's bothering you.

JILL: Why shouldn't it bother me? That's what I'm in the business of doing, isn't it? Making people laugh. And if they're not laughing . . .

HARRY: You need some new jokes. You're tired of doing the same ones every night. They're old.

JILL: All comedians tell old jokes. Mine are no older than anyone else's.

HARRY: Well, they're not getting the laughs, so what are you going to do about it?

JILL: What d'ye expect me to do? What can I do?

HARRY: It's becoming more difficult to book you into places, Jill. The kind of places that you want to be booked into. It's never been that easy but . . .

JILL: (*Interrupting*) What d'ye mean 'never'?

HARRY: Not since I've been doing the job.

JILL: My other managers didn't have much trouble.

19

HARRY: It's a wonder they didn't stick around then, isn't it?

JILL: I got rid of them. They didn't get rid of me . . . With one exception.

HARRY: If you'd take my advice things'd be a lot better.

JILL: Are we back to bowel function again?

HARRY: No, we're not.

JILL: I'm sick of hearing your advice.

HARRY: (*Angry*) Well, what d'ye pay me for? Am I guaranteed audience, is that it? You'll have one customer no matter what.

JILL: You know what I pay you for.

HARRY: I don't. I used to. I thought I knew.

JILL: I pay you to do as you're told. To do the things I can't be bothered doing . . . like buying bananas. You haven't even bought me a bloody banana.

HARRY: Buy your own bloody bananas.

JILL: It's your job. I can't go on stage without a banana.

HARRY: You could use a plastic banana.

JILL: So could you.

HARRY: It'd be less trouble all round.

JILL: I only want a banana. A bloody banana. Is that too much to ask, a banana?

HARRY: Bananas are out of season.

JILL: They were in season yesterday.

HARRY: Well, they're out of season today.
(*Short pause.*)

JILL: Sometimes I think you don't love me.

HARRY: I can only supply bananas when I'm in the mood.

JILL: Sod off, then, and get in the mood. I can rehearse without you.

HARRY: The management wants me to stay. I could do with a laugh.

JILL: Please yourself . . . I have been working on some new material actually. It's dedicated to you.

HARRY: Well, let's hear it.

(JILL *takes a few seconds to change from talking to rehearsing*.)

JILL: I'd like to say a word to the ladies now. Men! What use are they? (*To a member of the audience.*) Is yours any good, love? Are his parts in working order? Can you see when he's sitting like that? . . . get him to stand up. I'm looking for a new model myself. Mine wear out. I replace them all the time . . . they've been superseded really, haven't they? Who needs a man these days when you can see to your own fuse box?

HARRY: Very funny.

JILL: Who asked you?

HARRY: If I was in the audience I'd want my money back.

(JILL *ignores* HARRY *and continues to rehearse.*)

JILL: Look at that feller over there. He's only got one ear. Never mind, love, at least you're different . . . Well, not different. Peculiar. I'm not embarrassing you, am I? You're probably better off with the one. Less wax . . . having two of something isn't necessarily an improvement. What you find, to be perfectly honest, is that one of them is always better than the other. More use to you . . . I've got two children. One of them is better than the other. Slightly. It'll be measurable on some scientific scale. David is three milligrams better than Miriam. Mainly due to the fact that he lives further away. New Zealand. He does something with sheep. I'm sure they enjoy it. He was rather upset about the Common Market. He must've thought I had something to do with it because he hasn't written to me since. Oh, well. Family life! What fun!

(*Pause.*)

HARRY: He doesn't live in New Zealand.

JILL: Who does?

HARRY: You're going to carry on in that vein, are you, all night?

JILL: Don't you like it?

21

HARRY: No.

JILL: It'll sound better with an audience.

HARRY: Not if they're anything like last night's.

JILL: I don't want to hear about last night's.

HARRY: The management don't want it to happen again.

JILL: Do they think I do?

HARRY: You'll have to give them something better than that.
(*Short pause.*)

JILL: Last night's audience were pigs.

HARRY: Yes, but they were pigs who wanted entertaining.

JILL: You said it yourself—a bit of leg, that's all they were
interested in.

HARRY: Show them yours. You used to.

JILL: Have you seen my legs lately? It'd be the best laugh of
the night. I've no desire to make a spectacle of myself.

HARRY: The management aren't at all happy . . .

JILL: I'm not at all happy.

HARRY: They don't want to embarrass you . . .
(JILL *waits for* HARRY *to continue.*)

HARRY: . . . but they're thinking of asking someone else to
step in . . . You can say you're unwell.
(*Pause.*)

JILL: Can I?

HARRY: Yes.
(*Short pause.*)

JILL: What's in it for you?

HARRY: Does there have to be something in it for me?

JILL: If you've got some kind of deal going, Harry, just tell
me. I admire opportunists. I didn't get where I am
today without pushing and shoving.

HARRY: Where are you today, Jill?

JILL: At the minute I'm in a doss-house in some town that
means nothing to me. It may be heart and home and
mind to many thousands of people but I don't even
know its name. I've been in this place for years.

(*Short pause.*)

HARRY: I think you're suffering from depression. It's your age.

JILL: Age has nothing to do with it.

HARRY: You've all got the same thing wrong with you, you women. I've never met one yet that . . .

JILL: That what?

HARRY: Nothing. I suppose it's something men don't understand.

JILL: It could be anything, then.

(*Short pause.*)

HARRY: You're not as good as you thought you were. That's the problem.

JILL: Is it?

HARRY: You've been successful, Jill, but you were never a top star.

JILL: I was. I can show you billboards with my name on, big. Underlined. I got whatever fee I asked for.

HARRY: You had your moments.

JILL: I had more than moments. If they were moments, what did anyone else have? I don't understand you. What are you trying to say? What's on your mind?

HARRY: You know I think a lot of you.

(JILL *gives a derisory shrug.*)

HARRY: I don't want to see you look a fool.

JILL: I'm a professional fool.

HARRY: Last night's audience . . .

JILL: Don't tell me about last night's audience.

HARRY: Last night's audience . . .

JILL: I don't want to know!

HARRY: Last night's audience walked out.

JILL: They didn't.

HARRY: They might as well've done. You were talking to yourself.

JILL: Was I?

HARRY: You were very easy to ignore.

23

JILL: I wasn't on form last night.

HARRY: Nobody laughed.

JILL: I can't make them laugh. People've laughed before. They've laughed for years. They laughed the night before last night.

HARRY: The whole week's been a disaster.

JILL: You booked it.

HARRY: I book you into places that suit you. That suit your style.

JILL: You book me into second-rate clubs.

HARRY: You're a second-rate act.

JILL: I'm not. I usedn't to be.

HARRY: You've had your season. You can't go on for ever.

JILL: No one'd be any good here. You can't even shit in the place.

HARRY: Jill, I've checked the record. You had your high spots. People courted you. Everybody smiled at you once. But it was short-lived. You can't get it back. It's gone.

JILL: You said this wasn't a bad patch.

HARRY: It's not a bad patch. This is what it's like.

JILL: There's more.

HARRY: There's not.

JILL: D'you know what I went through to be what I am today? D'ye know what I gave up? What I didn't bother with?

HARRY: I've got some idea.

JILL: I put everything into this. If it's not in my act, then I haven't got it. I don't know it. It doesn't exist.

HARRY: It's all a bit old hat.

JILL: I can't be reborn. I'm the age that I am.

HARRY: It's not a question of being reborn. It's a question of accepting your limitations.

JILL: I haven't got any.

HARRY: It's too late in the day for adolescent dreams . . .

24

You've done all you're going to do.

JILL: I haven't.

HARRY: We've all got to come to terms with things. I used to think I was going to do hell and all. I'd make a million. I'd be a big businessman. And look at me now.

JILL: It's that bad, is it, being with me?

HARRY: No, I've got a roof over my head. I've got money in my pocket. It's not everything I ever wanted, though.

JILL: Well, bugger off and get everything you ever wanted then. Don't think I'm stopping you.

HARRY: All I'm saying is I know my capabilities. You should know yours.

JILL: No wonder I'm working in second-rate clubs. You'll have me playing the spoons outside picture houses next.

HARRY: They're 'entertainment centres' now.

JILL: Sorry.

HARRY: I'm being realistic. You ought to try it.

JILL: No thanks. (*Indicating the audience.*) They're the realistic ones, that lot. They know what to do. They know where they're going. They can tell you the interest rate, and how many miles to expect to the gallon. They've got their credit limit written down somewhere. That's them. That's what audiences are for.

HARRY: And what are you for? Can you tell me that? Because lately I've lost track of it completely.

JILL: Harry, I'm fifty-two . . . Everything below the waist has a will of its own.

HARRY: I don't know what I'm supposed to do these days.

JILL: I bleed all the time now.

HARRY: There must be something that'll stop it.

JILL: The Grand Coulee dam.

HARRY: It couldn't be that bad.

JILL: How would you know? I'm talking about things you haven't got.

HARRY: I have been sick once or twice.

JILL: I'm not sick . . . I'm . . . changing.

HARRY: Other women manage.

JILL: There's nothing solid inside me.

HARRY: What about some more pads, or cotton wool, or something?

JILL: Oh, for God's sake.

HARRY: I'm trying to be helpful.

JILL: Don't bother.

HARRY: Look, perhaps it would be a good idea if you didn't go on tonight. You couldn't really feel like performing.

JILL: What'll I do if I don't perform? Sit in some hotel room?

HARRY: You'd be more comfortable.

JILL: Would I?

HARRY: We could have an early night.

JILL: With a wad of cotton wool between us?

HARRY: Well, if you're not well.

JILL: Harry, I know you're doing a deal behind my back. Every manager I've ever had has pulled some stunt or other in the end, but will you just tell me what it is? If it's over between us that's OK, but let it finish amicably.

HARRY: I'm not doing a deal.

JILL: I can't stand being lied to.

HARRY: I'm not lying.

JILL: You're in that office all the time. What's going on?

HARRY: I told you. They want to bring someone else in. You can hardly blame them after last night.

JILL: Last night was the worst night of my life. They were more interested in their chicken-in-the-basket than in me. I hate audiences who eat.

HARRY: They don't want you to go on again. They're starting to get nasty about it . . . This other girl, she's up and coming.

JILL: People went to the toilet during my act.

HARRY: You can't stop their bodily functions.

JILL: Can't I?

26

HARRY: What d'you want to be billed as? The act that blocks intestines?

JILL: Yes.

HARRY: Is it worth fighting over? One show?

JILL: It's my show.

HARRY: They can get someone else. It won't matter. Go back to the dressing room and rest . . .

JILL: I don't like dressing rooms. I prefer it here.

HARRY: Maurice might want to rehearse.

JILL: I'm not moving out for him. I'm not a mad woman to be holed up in some corner of the attic.

HARRY: Don't get excited.

JILL: They booked me for the whole week. It's in the contract.

HARRY: I know it is.

JILL: They can't ignore that.

HARRY: They can be awkward.

JILL: This has never happened to me before.

HARRY: You've had a good run. You've made a mint of money. Most people've heard of you. That's why they booked you here in the first place. You're not unknown. You've always produced a good show.

(*Short pause.*)

JILL: Have I? People've walked out of every performance I ever gave. Usually it's to catch the last bus. Or so I tell myself. But I don't know. I can't shout after them. I can't say: 'Why are you leaving? Have you heard all this? Was it on somewhere last week?' I can't find out what people don't like. They just turn their backs.

HARRY: I know it's difficult.

JILL: It's awful this fear of boring people.

HARRY: Well, have a night off.

JILL: I keep wondering if I'd laugh.

HARRY: Of course you would.

JILL: Would I?

27

HARRY: Yes. You're very funny.
(*Short pause.*)
JILL: Hold my hand, Harry.
HARRY: I will if you promise to rest.
JILL: I'll rest.
(JILL *takes* HARRY's *hand and then embraces him as if for comfort. After a few seconds enter* MIRIAM, *unseen. She watches.* JILL *and* HARRY *kiss.*)
HARRY: Go to the dressing room.
JILL: All right. I won't be long, though.
(*Exit* JILL. HARRY *pauses watching* JILL *exit.* HARRY *starts to tidy the stage but notices* MIRIAM.)
MIRIAM: That's all part of the act. Don't think it means anything.
HARRY: Miriam?
MIRIAM: Who else are you expecting?
HARRY: I wasn't sure if you'd . . .
MIRIAM: (*Interrupting*) I couldn't help seeing. I was watching . . . When I was a little girl I used to put my ear to the wall. It was always her manager then.
HARRY: Why didn't you say something?
MIRIAM: I never interrupt Mother's performances. Or anyone else's . . . You're young enough to be David. Does she shout at you for leaving your model aeroplanes all over the house?
HARRY: No.
MIRIAM: She was such a silly woman.
HARRY: Thanks for coming. She'll be glad to see you.
MIRIAM: They don't usually write to me. It was quite a surprise.
HARRY: I thought you should know how she was.
MIRIAM: Did you?
HARRY: I thought you'd understand better than David would.
MIRIAM: I doubt if I will.

HARRY: As long as one of you's here. I thought somebody ought to know.

MIRIAM: You know.

HARRY: Some member of her family.

MIRIAM: Well, insofar as she has a family, we're it. David's busy, though.

HARRY: I know she wrote to you herself. She said she had.

MIRIAM: Yes. The postman complained. Her letters are so heavy.

HARRY: Did she say she'd been ill?

MIRIAM: I don't know. David puts her letters in the bin. I like to burn mine.

HARRY: Why?

MIRIAM: I know everything she's liable to tell me. And I've seen her act. What more is there?

HARRY: You haven't seen her recently.

MIRIAM: No. But that's fine by me.

HARRY: She wants to see you. She's desperate to make contact again.

MIRIAM: D'you know why we don't see each other?

HARRY: No. She doesn't discuss all her personal business with me. There's a lot she keeps to herself. I've learnt not to probe.

(*Pause.*)

HARRY: Shall I tell her you've arrived?

MIRIAM: There's no hurry.

HARRY: Will you stay for the show?

MIRIAM: I've seen it.

HARRY: It's not just Jill. There are other acts.

MIRIAM: I've seen it.

(*Pause.* MIRIAM *looks around the stage.*)

HARRY: Are you looking for something?

MIRIAM: Yes.

HARRY: What?

(MIRIAM *doesn't answer. Pause.*)

29

HARRY: You haven't got a banana on you, have you?

MIRIAM: Not that I know of.

(*Short pause.*)

MIRIAM: She's been doing that for years. I didn't think people laughed at bananas any more.

HARRY: They don't. But she doesn't know when to stop.

MIRIAM: She never did.

HARRY: Things aren't going well.

MIRIAM: I'm not surprised. Her act is very boring. The only time it wasn't boring was one evening when her dress caught fire.

HARRY: Really? She never told me about that. When was it?

MIRIAM: Oh, years ago. The orchestra leader put her out. She slept with him a couple of times afterwards. Whether it was his reward or his punishment he never knew.

HARRY: It's funny she hasn't mentioned it. You'd think she'd use it as one of her stories.

MIRIAM: She was embarrassed. It was the only night she stopped the show. Herself and a fire extinguisher.

HARRY: A lot of things've happened since then.

MIRIAM: She's non-combustible now, is she?

HARRY: She is as far as I'm concerned. She doesn't really need me for anything in particular. I kind of hang around.

MIRIAM: I wondered when she'd lose her grip.

HARRY: She's in decline. I keep telling her she isn't, but she is. The job's no use to me any more. But I don't like leaving her when she needs someone.

MIRIAM: She doesn't need me.

HARRY: She talks about you in her act. You must mean something to her.

MIRIAM: Don't you listen to her act? She hates the sight of me.

HARRY: She doesn't. She'll say anything for a laugh.

MIRIAM: She means every word. She's very truthful on stage. It's once she comes off that the trouble starts. I don't see

30

why you're bothered anyway.

HARRY: She's been good to me. I don't want to hurt her feelings. But I can't mess around like this much longer.

MIRIAM: She won't care. All her managers move on to better things. They could hardly do otherwise.

HARRY: She's very generous.

MIRIAM: Well, grab what's going and run. In a week she won't remember you. She can't even remember the ones she married. She's just a performer. They flit around, here, there. Keep on the move. They're only wanted for short periods. You know that yourself.

HARRY: I feel obligated to her.

MIRIAM: You can feel what you like. It won't make any difference when you leave.

HARRY: She's middle-aged and she's running to fat. Someone should take an interest.

MIRIAM: Someone will. But not me . . . I've only come because I've got something to tell her.
(*Short pause.*)

HARRY: She had a bad night last night.

MIRIAM: So did I.

HARRY: I don't think she should be upset any more.

MIRIAM: I used to be upset by faces peering through curtains. Shapes bedclothes made in the dark. A dog sat all night on my dressing table. But Mother took no notice. She was always in the next room. Performing. With people like you. I haven't come here to take part in her life. There's something that has to be said, that's all.

HARRY: Does it have to be said today?

MIRIAM: Yes. I've never been able to share anything with her before. Raymond thought we had nothing in common.

HARRY: Who's Raymond?

MIRIAM: One of your predecessors.
(*Short pause.*)

HARRY: They walked out on her last night.

31

MIRIAM: I'm sorry I missed it . . . Oh, is this her now, the star?

(*Enter* JILL, *agitated*.)

JILL: Harry, I've blocked the toilet again. It won't clear.

HARRY: I'll see to it. I used to be a plumber.

JILL: I asked Maurice to poke around with his baton. He might as well use it for something.

MIRIAM: Hello.

JILL: Miriam! Look, Harry! Look who's come.

MIRIAM: He has looked.

HARRY: She's just arrived.

MIRIAM: A few minutes ago.

JILL: Why didn't you tell me? . . . It's lovely to see you . . . It's been so long.

MIRIAM: Doesn't time fly?

JILL: It's lovely to see you.

HARRY: I'll fix the toilet.

JILL: No, don't. This is Miriam, Harry. This is my Miriam. You've heard me speak of her.

HARRY: Yes.

MIRIAM: I'm sure.

JILL: It's lovely to see you.

MIRIAM: So you said.

JILL: Have you met Harry? Have you had a talk to each other?

MIRIAM: Yes. He wrote to me. That's partly why I came. I knew where you were.

JILL: I wrote to you, too.

MIRIAM: Yes, that's right.

JILL: What did Harry write to you for?

HARRY: I told her you were sick.

JILL: I told her that myself.

HARRY: Well, I didn't know.

JILL: Why didn't you tell me you were writing to her?

MIRIAM: You could've put your letters in the same envelope.

Saved on the postage.

JILL: (*Change of tone*) Why were you writing to Miriam behind my back?

HARRY: I've told you. I wanted her to know you were sick.

JILL: I'm better now.

HARRY: Well, I'll write and tell her.

JILL: Don't be petulant.

HARRY: I'll unblock the toilet.

JILL: What's the matter with you, Harry?

HARRY: Nothing. You want the toilet unblocked. You can have it unblocked.

JILL: You don't have to shout at me.

HARRY: I'm not shouting.

JILL: I don't want Miriam to think you're uncouth.

HARRY: She doesn't.

JILL: That's no way to behave in front of people.

MIRIAM: He's not uncouth. He's not anything.

JILL: He's a nice boy.

MIRIAM: You're going in for younger ones.

JILL: Yes.

MIRIAM: Why?

JILL: Can we keep off that subject?

MIRIAM: No.

JILL: I'd like us to be friendly.

MIRIAM: Would you?

JILL: Yes. Yes, I would. Very much.

MIRIAM: It's too late.

JILL: (*Quietly*) It isn't.

(HARRY *makes as if to leave the stage*.)

JILL: (*Nervous*) Where are you going?

HARRY: You don't want me here.

JILL: I do.

MIRIAM: Mother and I don't like to be alone.

HARRY: You can talk better without me.

JILL: We can't.

33

HARRY: It's not me she's come to see.

JILL: Miriam, things have happened in the past that I never intended. When you've got a career to pursue you seem to overlook some aspects of . . .

MIRIAM: I'm not interested.

JILL: I know things haven't been right between us . . .

MIRIAM: Don't bother.

JILL: But we can make amends. I can make amends. I can forget . . .

MIRIAM: What?

JILL: Anything. Anything you want me to forget.

(*Pause.* JILL *is very tense. Exit* HARRY.)

JILL: I'm sorry I never buried your kitten!

MIRIAM: What kitten?

JILL: I didn't realize how much it meant to you. It was just a squelch in the road. I didn't take it seriously. You were always having hysterics over something. You were that kind of child.

MIRIAM: I'd forgotten all about the kitten.

JILL: If I'd realized how much it meant to you I would've buried it. I could've flushed it away, at least. It's efficient. It's a good way to go.

MIRIAM: It was only a kitten.

JILL: They're supposed to have nine lives.

MIRIAM: It was a substandard kitten.

JILL: And to be able to see in the dark.

MIRIAM: Maybe it could. You ran over it in broad daylight.

JILL: Did I?

MIRIAM: Yes.

JILL: Well, I'm sorry. I'm terribly sorry. I'll buy you a new one.

MIRIAM: Thanks.

(*Short pause.*)

JILL: Miriam, this isn't how I wanted it to be.

MIRIAM: No.

34

JILL: We've such a lot to say.

MIRIAM: I don't think I have.

JILL: I have. I always have had. I couldn't say it in the past. I always had to do things. I always had to go to places. I always had to entertain.

MIRIAM: Yes.

JILL: But I'm finally getting my priorities right.

MIRIAM: Are you?

JILL: Things are going to be different now.

MIRIAM: Yes, they are. For me, anyway.

JILL: I'll tell you the truth, Miriam. It hasn't gone well here. Everything's changing. It's not like it used to be. My points of reference don't mean anything any more. Not to these people. These are new people. I barely skim their surface. I cause ripples. It's not enough.

MIRIAM: This is nothing to me.

JILL: I can't make contact any more. When I come out on stage I'm deaf. I hear nothing. I'm aware of no reaction. I'm on my own.

MIRIAM: Yes.

JILL: Everything I relied on has gone to bits.

MIRIAM: Really?

JILL: Yes, that's why I want to put things right between us.

MIRIAM: You could never make me laugh.

JILL: I'm sorry for all the times I left you. I want to make amends.

MIRIAM: You can't.

JILL: I won't come between you and Raymond. You've nothing to fear there.

MIRIAM: I know I haven't.

JILL: You must've missed things, too. You never had a real mother. You could have one now. We could get to know each other.

MIRIAM: D'ye think that's what I want?

JILL: You came here.

35

MIRIAM: I didn't come for that.

JILL: Didn't you? When I saw you, I thought . . . I hoped.
  (*Short pause.*)

MIRIAM: Do you ever hear from David?

JILL: No.

MIRIAM: You really were successful, weren't you? You didn't
  want either of us, and eventually you got rid of both of
  us.

JILL: Things were different then.

MIRIAM: David's changed his name.

JILL: Has he? He didn't tell me.

MIRIAM: I think that's going to extremes. I don't see the
  point. But then he always went over the top. Like you.
  Full of grand gestures.

JILL: I didn't want to sit at home all the time. That's what
  women did in those days. Would you do it?

MIRIAM: Raymond's dead.

JILL: What?

MIRIAM: Raymond's dead. That's what I came to tell you.

JILL: What?

MIRIAM: He's dead. You must know what that means.

JILL: What d'ye mean he's dead?

MIRIAM: I mean he's dead. What else can I mean? What other
  word is there? He's not alive. He died. He's dead.

JILL: I don't believe you.

MIRIAM: Why not? It's not a difficult concept to grasp. People
  die all the time. Everyday. Everywhere. It's a wonder to
  me the streets aren't knee-deep in corpses. Everybody
  dies. Some day you'll be dead yourself. But Raymond's
  dead now.
  (*Pause.*)

JILL: Raymond's dead?

MIRIAM: Well, they put him in a box.

JILL: I don't understand.

MIRIAM: He was dead so they put him in a box. It was no

good leaving him there.

JILL: But what did he die of? There was nothing wrong with him, was there?

MIRIAM: His piles were always a trouble.

JILL: He can't be dead.

MIRIAM: Well, perhaps he will be by the time they've done the post-mortem.

(*Short pause.*)

JILL: Was it an accident?

MIRIAM: I suppose it depends on your philosophy of life.

JILL: Tell me how he died.

MIRIAM: I don't know exactly. I wasn't there at the time.

JILL: Where were you?

MIRIAM: I was in bed.

JILL: I thought he slept with you. I thought that was the whole point of your going off together. I thought that was the main thrust behind it all.

MIRIAM: It was.

JILL: I mean, you couldn't do without him when he was mine. You followed him everywhere when he was mine. You ran around after him when he was mine. You couldn't bear to be away from him when he was mine.

MIRIAM: Times change.

JILL: When he was mine he was wonderful. You'd love him forever. You'd give him everything.

MIRIAM: It all got a bit much.

JILL: You said you couldn't live without him.

MIRIAM: I was joking. I thought you'd laugh. I did like him. He was the best one you ever had. But slightly too old.

(*Short pause.*)

JILL: How did he die?

MIRIAM: He hanged himself. I found him behind the hall door like an old coat.

(*Pause.* JILL *is stunned.*)

MIRIAM: This is odd, I thought. I'd only gone to bring in the milk.

37

JILL: He hanged himself?

MIRIAM: He was swinging. Back and forth. Back and forth. Nice rhythm. Very soothing. Stocking feet. No shoes on. Shirt collar undone. What a surprise. What a surprise. I must tell Mother. I must tell Mother.

JILL: That's horrible.

MIRIAM: Yes. Isn't it?

(*Short pause.*)

JILL: I can't believe it. Why did he do it?

MIRIAM: He was depressed.

JILL: In what sense depressed?

MIRIAM: Commonly depressed. People get depressed.

JILL: I made him happy.

MIRIAM: For a while.

JILL: He never hanged himself when he was mine.

MIRIAM: Perhaps he was deranged . . . Anyway, you've got Harry now.

JILL: I don't want Harry.

MIRIAM: Come in Harry. Your time is up.

JILL: Raymond was the one who made me happy.

MIRIAM: Oh yes. Yes, of course.

JILL: You wouldn't understand.

MIRIAM: No, I wouldn't. I thought they all made you happy. That's what it seemed like to me. One after the other. Something new every night.

JILL: It wasn't like that.

MIRIAM: A new town. A new audience. A new manager. The same jokes. The constant in a changing world.

JILL: People used to think I was funny.

MIRIAM: They used to laugh at you.

JILL: Raymond had faith in me . . . Not like Harry. He wants me to give up. He doesn't want me to go on.

MIRIAM: You will, though, won't you?

JILL: I don't know . . . I feel sick.

MIRIAM: I can't understand why the newspapers haven't been

38

to see you. Suicide's always good for a paragraph. And a theatrical suicide ought to rate half a column . . . D'ye think even they're not interested any more? Hasn't even the local paper come?

(*Short pause.*)

JILL: Why didn't you stop him?

MIRIAM: I didn't know he was going to do anything . . . I said goodnight. I usually went to bed first. We'd grown predictable . . . That was all. As I left the room he took off his tie.

JILL: He must've said something.

MIRIAM: He didn't. What could he've said? 'Miriam, I've bought a rope. I'm about to hang myself'? He said goodnight. When you intend to do something, you just do it.

(*Enter* HARRY.)

HARRY: I know you've got things to say to each other. I don't like to interrupt but I've got the management breathing down my neck . . . Jill, they don't want you to go on tonight. They're adamant. I know it's harsh saying it like that, but we've got to be realistic. You could be ill on stage. Anything . . . Let this new girl have a go. It's only one performance. I've just seen her do some stuff. She's OK. The audience'll be happy enough. It's safer. You look awful anyway. The rest'll do you good. You'll feel better tomorrow . . . They'll pay you full money. They don't want any trouble. This new girl won't cost them much. She hasn't had your experience . . . So I'll tell them that's OK, shall I?

JILL: Raymond's dead.

HARRY: Oh, is he? Well, that's all right, then. It works out quite well. You won't want to perform anyway, will you?

JILL: He thought I was a good comic.

HARRY: So did a lot of people, but I suppose most of them are dead. That's the way it goes.

39

JILL: He said I was original, years ago.

HARRY: I suppose you were, years ago . . . I'll tell them that's all right, shall I? We can go back to the hotel. Maurice wants to rehearse here.

MIRIAM: I think I will stay for the show. I need to laugh . . . I've made my statement. They know my version of events. They won't need me now till the inquest. Apparently I've got to identify him, seeing as he can no longer identify himself. I might as well stay here with the bright lights. There's nothing for me anywhere else . . . I can't go home any more than you can go to your hotel room.

HARRY: What does she mean?

JILL: I'm not standing down. Even Miriam knows that.

HARRY: It's only one performance. What difference does it make?

MIRIAM: I'll sit near the stage. I want to hear every word.

(MIRIAM *starts to leave, but looks back at* JILL.)

MIRIAM: Your breasts sag.

JILL: Yours stick out the back.

MIRIAM: Goodbye.

(*Exit* MIRIAM.)

HARRY: I've given my word . . . They don't want you.

JILL: I don't care what they want.

HARRY: What about what I want?

JILL: A bit of blood was enough to turn you off. A layer of extra flesh.

HARRY: You are a lot older than I am.

JILL: It's not just years.

HARRY: I've got a chance here with these people. If you mess it up for me . . .

JILL: I've never gone on stage for anyone's benefit but my own. And I won't come off stage for anyone either. Not you. Not Miriam. Not Raymond.

HARRY: I hope your performance stinks. I hope you're booed

off. I hope you're ignored.

JILL: Thank you.

HARRY: You were always a solo act.

JILL: That's right. I'm very vivid in the head. If I want you, I can imagine you.

HARRY: I'll be down there watching.

(*He indicates the audience*.)

JILL: I hope you enjoy it.

HARRY: I will.

(*Exit* HARRY. *Exit* JILL.)

ACT TWO

Musical introduction.

VOICE: And now, ladies and gentlemen, put your hands
together for the star of our show, Miss Jill Jeffers.
(*Applause. Enter* JILL, *dressed for the stage. When she's doing
her 'legitimate' act, she can use a more common accent, 'old-
fashioned'.*)

JILL: Thank you, thank you, thank you. Good evening, ladies
and gentlemen. My name is Jill Jeffers and I've come
here tonight to entertain you.
(*More applause. The above speech is a kind of signature tune
which the audience has been expecting.*)
I hope you're ready for a laugh. You are? Well, I know a
little place around the corner, you've still got time to get
to . . . no, I'm only joking. Stay where you are. You
know me, Jill Jeffers—the biggest thing about her is her
smile. That's what they used to say. Wouldn't say it
now, though. The biggest thing about her is her hip
measurement. A hundred and one. Metric, that is.
Everything sounds bigger in French, doesn't it?

Are any of you a hundred and one round here? (*She
demonstrates her hips*) . . . No? . . . You're trying to make
out that I'm the fattest person in the room. Well, me and
that woman stuck in the doorway . . . It's a hard life,
isn't it? I tried everything when I was young to get rid of
some weight. Did no good—all I ever lost was my
virginity. I think I left it on the top deck of a bus one
time. It was either that or my plastic mac. You forget

42

the details as you grow older . . . I missed it, though. You know what the British summers are like.

Look at these legs. They're like a pair of Californian redwoods. I found a squirrel storing nuts in them once. I won't say where.

Oh God, have you seen my overhanging ankles? I haven't got a spare tyre: it's an inflatable life-raft . . . and my double chin . . . It's not fat, you know . . . It's water . . . If you put your hand on my stomach (*She demonstrates*) there, just there—press it in a bit, and swivel it around—oh, I'll give you a go later—you know what it feels like? One of those plastic bags you win at the fair with a goldfish in. It does, you know. You'd think that was what it was. Mind you, you could get more than a goldfish in there these days. The size of it now, it'd take a couple of fresh salmon. Half a dozen trout.

Listen, there's that much water in my body I'm thinking of fitting flippers on my vitals. I believe a lot of fellers go for that nowadays. It turns them on . . . There's no accounting for taste, like, as the man said when he kissed the cow.

Your body lets you down though, doesn't it? If my gums recede any further, my eyes'll drop out. Oooooh, the things I regret doing with my body! . . . Like smoking. Smoking's knocked years off my life. I'm fifty-two. If I hadn't smoked, I'd be sixty-six. You've got to laugh.

I've just come out of hospital actually. I had a certain operation. Quite unusual in a woman of my age. I bet some of you've had it, though. It's fairly common in young people apparently, although they don't always do what I did because attitudes are changing. Every case is assessed on its merits. So they say. But I got mine done quick enough. No messing. You're only in a day. I said to the surgeon afterwards, 'How long before I can have sexual relations?' He said, 'I've got no idea, love. You're the first patient who's asked me that after a tonsillectomy.'

Ah, but you can't trust doctors nowadays, can you? They do what they like with you. There was a nice young feller on the ward I was on, though. He said to me one morning, 'I've just brought in two cases of dysentery.' I said to him, 'Well, that's very kind of you, darling, but I'll stick to the Lucozade if it's all the same to you.' You've got to laugh.

What I don't like about doctors is the way they start writing the prescription as you walk through the door. I know a woman went to the doctor to get a coil fitted. Came out with a hearing-aid . . . they'll put anything anywhere. They don't care.

(*Short pause.* JILL *says the next lines as if pretending to the audience that they are jokes a comedian has to tell, by virtue of being a comedian, even though they're not very funny.*)

Oh, God! What's green and pear-shaped? . . . A pear.

What's green and pear-shaped and splattered on the floor? . . . A peardrop.

I thought that one up myself. I didn't pinch it off any other comic. Well, you wouldn't would you? If any other comic had that joke, I'd be quite happy to leave it with him.

What d'ye call a septic cat? . . . Puss.

A Greek washing-up liquid? . . . Plato.

How about an Englishman, a Frenchman and a Yank in the middle of the ocean? . . . Nato.

It's a gift being able to think of these. It is, you know. I got it free in a packet of Sugar Puffs.

Did I ever tell you about my Uncle Henry? . . . Sad story. He was only a young man. Died of asbestosis. Took us six months to cremate the body. You've got to laugh.

You can get a laugh out of death, can't you? You know what they say about old fishermen? They never die: they always smell like that.

Oh God, I suppose I've insulted some fisherman in the audience. I'm not kidding, you've got to be so careful these days. You can't tell Irish jokes, you can't tell Asian jokes, you can't tell spastic, mongol, cross-eyed, hunchback, one leg longer than the other jokes. Who's left? Personally, I can't see anything wrong with having one leg longer than the other. It's better than having one leg shorter than the other.

Men have always been good for a laugh, though, haven't they? I must've thought so once or I wouldn't've kept marrying them. Mind you, as it turned out, the only thing I ever had in common with most of my husbands was the cake and the photograph album . . . Well, how would you feel on your wedding night? You're all propped up in bed—see-through nightie, no rollers, you've had a wash down—and there he is getting undressed—this happened to me, it really did—when out from under his shirt falls a piece of paper: batteries not included. Jees.

And they think they're God's gift, don't they? Women are much better. Friend of mine went on a day trip to heaven once. (*As if contradicting*) She did, you know. Booked it with the LRT. Anyway, when she got there, God was sorting out the new intake. 'All the men who've been henpecked by their wives,' he said, 'queue up on the left. And all the men who haven't been henpecked, queue up on the right.' About three hundred big, burly men went and stood on the left, and one little feller, six stone, pigeon-chest, knock-knees—this isn't ethnic, honest—stood on the right. So God went over to him. 'Pull the other one,' he said. 'This is the queue for the men who haven't been henpecked. Why are you standing here?' 'My wife told me to,' he said.

And that's typical of them, isn't it? Do as they're told so long as it suits them. My first husband was like that . . . Oh, when I think of it. I was a sweet, young thing then. I was a child bride. So was he . . . it was a white wedding: we were both terrified. The first night was a disaster. He told me what he knew, and I told him what I knew. I'll never forget the look on his face. 'You've just made that up,' he said. 'Haven't you?'

Of course, the whole bloody relationship was a failure. I don't know why I did it. He used to lie in bed at night and kiss me. It was very dull. And very wet and slobbery. It gave me bad skin here round my mouth. I used to have to stop and wipe it off on the sheet. Best bit of the whole thing. I haven't seen him, now, for years. Donkeys years. I wouldn't know him any more. Well, I presume I wouldn't, though I might if he kissed me. Funny thing life, isn't it?

His name was Bill, or Will, or Phil, or Ill. I don't know. Something like that. It rhymed, anyway. Will Hill, or Phil Mill, or Bill Lill, or something. I've got no memory for detail. But he was no thrill. I don't know that they ever are. I mean, one of the others, God, d'ye know what he did? You wouldn't believe it. He bought me a set of saucepans. I don't mean he bought a set of saucepans. I mean he bought me a set of saucepans. For my birthday. I didn't know what to do with them. I thought it was . . . like . . . sports equipment. I thought you had to hit something with them. I kept looking for the ball. And he didn't seem to crack on, that was the thing.

All my husbands've been like that. A bit of a disappointment. There was the one who died. Of all the days he could've snuffed it, he had to choose one the

46

week before my Royal Command Performance. I
suppose ultimately it was of no real consequence. I
didn't have a ticket for him anyway. And the publicity
was good. Put me centre stage so to speak. I closed the
first half of the show. The Queen admired my
professionalism. And I admired hers . . . Mind you, I
almost didn't make it. He was being buried that same
afternoon. I had to go. Put in an appearance . . . and
someone had had the bright idea of bringing the body
home. A little romantic touch. First time we'd been
under the same roof together for months. Of course, the
undertaker arsed around. You'd've thought I had all the
time in the world. I kept saying to him, 'Will you put a
move on? I'm in a hurry.' But he just supped his whisky
and said, 'There's still a few minutes.' Well, there was,
but I didn't want him hanging around. I mean, they
didn't freeze the bodies in those days. The bloody man
was still fresh.

And then one of his relatives barged in. 'Oh my God!'
she said. 'He looks as healthy now as when he was alive.'
'Is that a fact?' I said. 'Well let me say one thing: I no
longer care what he looks like. All I know is, dead or
alive, he goes out of here at three o'clock.'

Life's a joke, isn't it? And someone's laughing. It's a
pity he hasn't come tonight. Whoever he is.
(*Short pause.*)
It's not as difficult as it seems, this, you know. Lots of
people can stand up on stage and tell jokes. They kid
you up it's hard but it's not so bad. Particularly if you
can't do anything else. And let's face it, you've got to do
something to pass the time if it's only sit in a chair and
breath. This is all I can do. I can't dance. I'm not
artistic. I can barely sing. I'm not musical at all . . . Did
you hear the one about Beethoven? . . . No, neither did
he. Beethoven was so deaf he thought he was a mime

47

artist. A feller told me once he was a government
artist—drew the dole. I said to him, 'Oh really. I
thought you had something wrong with your bladder.'

But it's a good job we're not all the same, isn't it?
You're not even like the other members of your family,
are you? I'll be glad when this genetic engineering comes
in. I'm putting myself down for two robots and a
clockwork mouse. Less trouble all round.

Actually, I've got two robots already. Have I told you
about them? They're the reason I'm the way I am today.
Insanity's hereditary. You get it off your kids. Well, you
do if they're anything like mine. They're twins. One's
identical, one isn't. But they're the same sex—a boy and
a girl. Well, a man and a woman really. I can't tell them
apart. I never could. He's the one who used to have
'David' on a piece of sellotape around his wrist. But they
don't make sellotape like they used to. After a couple of
years it was anybody's guess.

I gave him everything he ever wanted. When he was a
boy he had dinky cars. And Meccano. He sailed boats in
the bath. He liked six-guns and penknives and
pea-shooters. He was a macho-baby: he smashed up his
sister's dolls. It was through him I learned the value of
unbreakable toys. You use them for breaking up
breakable toys. He was a vicious little sod. And that's a
mother talking.

(*Pause.* JILL *is thinking about* DAVID *but rouses herself to launch
into* MIRIAM.)

The other one was as bad. Miriam. Miriam's a girl's
name in case you didn't know. Some people've never
heard of it. It's a derivative of Mary, meaning
'wished-for child'. I didn't know that when I had her.
David means 'beloved'.

Actually, I called her Miriam in the hope that she
might think her father was Jewish. He wasn't. But I

thought she'd be more likely to develop some business sense with a name like that. In the event, however, she's finished up with nothing but a distaste for sausages and the Jewish ability to look a gift-horse in the mouth. That's a reference to the history of Revelation in case there are any pagans here tonight. It comes to something when you have to explain your jokes.

Not that I was ever any good at explaining. Not to Miriam anyway. She always wanted to know where I was. Why I wasn't there. 'Jesus,' I'd say. 'I can't be in two places at once. I'm a comedian not a bloody magician. A bloody illusionist. If I'm making people laugh, I haven't got time for pushing you and your pram along the road. Why didn't you want a bicycle like David? David's independent. You can't even steer the pram properly. Your dolls keep falling out of it. Can't you strap the damn things in? Oh, they're a bloody nuisance, these bloody dolls. Miriam, for God's sake, watch the kerb. You're walking right off the goddam kerb. I'm not shouting at you. Why can't you be like David? Why can't you ride a bike? . . . Stop crying, for God's sake. I'm not shouting at you. I'm not. God, you're enough to make anybody shout. Look at David. He's alright. What's the matter with you? Will you stop crying? Will you stop that bloody crying? For God's sake, Miriam, will you shut up? You're driving me mad. I'm insane with the noise. Stop it. Stop it! I'm warning you. This is your last chance, or I'll . . .'

Oh, that kid! David could ride a bike. She wouldn't even try. 'I want my dolls. I want my dolls.' She was always standing against the wall clutching a doll to her breast. Chest. Silly cow. 'It's bloody plastic,' I'd say. 'Look, you can put your fingers in its eyes. You can pull its arms off. I'll show you . . . Yes, I know it wets itself, but you can pull its arms off. What sort of a love-object

49

is that? For Christ's sake, Miriam, stick this jelly baby in your mouth and shut up . . . I've got a joke about jelly babies, Miriam. D'ye want to hear it? How d'ye tell the legitimate jelly babies from the illegitimate jelly babies? Hey, Miriam, how d'ye do that? . . . You turn the bag upside down and the bastards fall out.'

(*Pause.*)

D'ye know what she did to spite me? She learned to play the piano. Classical pieces. She got her grade eight. She was always on about her grade eight. And later it was her advanced driving. Mind you, I wouldn't go in a car with her. Bloody woman couldn't manoeuvre a pram. What's she going to be like in a car?

(*Short pause.*)

When I think of what he got off with, that man. When I think of what I went through and he didn't. It's not the giving birth. You can get over that. It's being expected to care tuppence afterwards.

I entered Miriam for a charming child contest once. There were only eight kids in it. She came ninth. I know that isn't true. But it's how I feel.

Oh God, somebody, give us a song. Stick 10 pence in Maurice's navel and let's have a bit of music.

(JILL *sings loudly and brashly.*)

Oh, the sun was shining on the old pretty wall,
When the muck man fell in a fit.
And he cried, 'Hey, Mother, will you come and pull me out
Cause I'm up to my eyes in shit.'

(JILL *speaks again.*)

Oh shit. That's all you get out of kids, isn't it? Mind you, you didn't get it out of Miriam. She was forever constipated. She found it it very difficult to let go of anything once she had it in her grasp. As I know to my cost.

(JILL *makes a deliberate effort to change the mood*.)
Have I introduced you to Maurice, ladies and
gentlemen? He's the musical director around here. He's
the God figure if you like. We don't see him but we know
he's there. He's not very active in our affairs and
occasionally we even doubt his existence. But we'll hear
an uncalled-for trumpet blast now and then, or a waltz
in march time. Some minor disaster. Our creator saying
hello.

He's a very talented man of course. Not musically,
although I don't suppose you need me to tell you that.
His wife's just left him, apparently. He says he can't
understand why: he's got fitted carpet everywhere . . .
But we all have our cross to bear.

Maurice and I have been having a little contretemps
during the week, haven't we, darling? (*To the audience*) A
contretemps? Don't you know what that is? It's a
difference of opinion. A tiff. A disagreement. A bloody
great row. Maurice has been a pain in the arse since the
day I got here. No wonder your wife left you, Maurice.
No wonder she went off with the binman, or the
coalman, or whoever it was. No wonder she got out from
under before you bored her to death. Living with
Maurice, audience, must be about as exciting as
watching an iceberg melt . . . No, well, maybe not as
exciting as that. But similar.

I'm not joking, audience, I caught rigor mortis off
Maurice earlier in the week. Well, that was what the
doctor said it was . . . I was surprised too. Because I
thought that was a sexually-transmitted disease. I mean,
I got it off each of my husbands, not to mention one or
two others. But there you go. We live and learn.

I doubt if you could get anything transmitted off
Maurice. Not even if you plugged him into the mains
and threw a bucket of water over him. Some people are

51

simply inert. They don't actually do anything. I've been waiting for Maurice to show himself all week. I've been at this club six nights now, during which time he's had ample opportunity to take hold of his baton and demonstrate his prowess. Or, alternatively, he could've conducted the band. I'd've enjoyed either. Up to fairly recently I'd've enjoyed both. But I'm at a difficult age now. Aren't we all?

You come to a point in life where people don't look at you the same way any more. Men digging ditches don't whistle. A wolf cub offered to carry my bag the other day. I nearly hit him . . . I tell jokes about the war, but sometimes I wonder if people know which war I'm talking about. I thought there was only one, really. And it was a good laugh, wasn't it? I could tell you a joke about the war if it's not too old-fashioned. If it's not beneath you. Takes place in the middle of the blitz. Shells exploding all over. One old man was very slow to get out of the house and into the air raid shelter—Oh, you could change that to nuclear shelter and tell this joke in thirty years time. 'Come on, Grandad,' someone shouted. 'Hurry up.' 'I can't,' he yelled. 'I can't find my teeth.' 'Oh, bugger your teeth,' the other feller shouted back. 'They're dropping bombs, not sandwiches.'

I know it's not hysterical, but it's OK. It's the sort of thing they laughed at years ago. And there's nothing wrong with that. We all stand on the shoulders of previous generations. I know that's been said before, as well, but that doesn't make it untrue. Far from it. I can't go on writing new jokes. I could do it once. I did it for years. All that must count for something. For God's sake, I am fifty-two. I'm not exactly a babe in arms. Can't you give my past some credit? I was slim once. I had a good figure. A figure like a nigger, only bigger.

But you can't say that any more. A figure like Trigger only bigger . . . Trigger's a horse. A bloody horse. You remember Roy Rogers, don't you? And Gene Autrey? She had a nice voice . . . Well, I know they're all past it now, but what difference does that make? Some people never get up to it.

If you don't want to laugh, don't. I can take it. I've had knocks before. Life hasn't been that easy. What d'ye think it was like when I had those babies? David was first. Out like a shot. And then the afterbirth. No problem. It's fashionable to eat that nowadays, you know. Placenta and chips. Very tasty. They do it at the Chinese up the road. Ask for number 36 . . . I thought that was it. I thought it was over. 'And again,' they said. 'What?' I said. 'There's more?' 'Oh yes,' they said. 'There's another.' 'Oh, God,' I said. 'Isn't one enough? Can't you just plaster over the crack?' . . . But out she came, fists clenched, screaming and crying, bringing God knows what with her. What a performance. What a performance . . .

(JILL *now makes an attempt to fight off the mood she has got herself into.*)

Oh, God, Maurice, do something, will you? Play me that song. (*To the audience*) It's one about bananas. It seems appropriate somehow, I don't know. I used to sing it years ago. Come on, Maurice, it's in 4/4 time. One, two, three—

(JILL *sings, with music:*)*

Standing by the fruit stall on the corner
Once I heard a customer complain
You never seem to show

---

*'I Like Bananas (Because They Have No Bones)' is published by Chappell Music Ltd.

The fruit we all love so
That's why business hasn't been the same.

I don't like your peaches
They are full of stones
I like bananas
Because they have no bones.

Don't give me tomatoes
Can't stand ice cream cones
I like bananas
Because they have no bones

No matter where I go
With Susie, May or Anna,
I want the world to know
I must have my banana.

Cabbages and onions
Hurt my singing tones
I like bananas
Because they have no bones.
I like bananas because they have no bones.

(JILL *speaks again.*)
Great, wasn't it? . . . I know I got a bit over-emotional
before, ladies and gentlemen. You'll have to forgive me.
It's been that sort of a day. One thing after another.

But it's all good experience. You can't be up if you're
never down. D'ye know the one thing in the world I
wouldn't do? Ever. No matter what. Cycle round
Holland . . . The rest of Europe's OK. In fact we've got
family connections there through my Father. His legs are
in France. Just his legs. The rest of him's over here . . .
He lost his legs in the war . . . I know a joke about losing

54

your legs. It's very funny. An Irish feller—well, he mightn't've been Irish—stepped on a bomb. 'Paddy, Paddy,' he shouted to his mate, 'I've lost my legs.' 'No you haven't,' he said, 'they're over there.' Anyway, my old feller lost his. They were blown off. It was the First World War. Lots of people had legs blown off. The best you can say about it is no one lost more than two.

It made a difference, though. But not to me because I never knew him any other way. He was three feet two inches tall. Except one day when he fell out of his wheelchair. Then he was three feet two inches long. You've got to laugh, haven't you?

People used to talk to him in a loud voice as if he was deaf. As though when his legs had come away from his body, they'd stuffed themselves down his ears. For some reason. I drew a picture of him once like that, with big legs sticking out the sides of his head. My mother went mad, but he saw the joke. He was a comic . . . I used to lie awake at night and wonder where his legs had gone. I used to visualize them stuck in a tree, or maybe one fell down somebody's chimney. I could conceive of a *fermier* in northern France coming across them one day in a field of turnips. As they must.

(*She acts out picking up a leg.*)

Oh, mais, qu'est-ce que c'est? . . . It's amazing the things you leave behind you. They'll be dug up eventually by archaeologists. He'll probably be pieced together in millenniums to come. Or is it millennia?

(*Pause.*)

Oh, God, this is depressing, isn't it? . . . I'm sorry, ladies and gentlemen. I don't know what's the matter with me tonight . . . Maurice, have you got that other song? The one Vera used to sing? . . . Yes, Vera. Vera Lynn.

(JILL *sings without waiting for the music.*)

Send for the midwife, Mary,

Something in my belly's gone pop.

(JILL *speaks again.*)

Yes, Vera sang that. Don't you remember? Only she used to sing it and bang a big bass drum at the same time.

(JILL *sings again and bangs a bass drum.*)

    Send for the midwife, bang,
    Something in my belly's gone bang.

(JILL *speaks.*)

She won't crack on about it now, but that's what she did. And what's wrong with it? If that's what you have to do to get yourself noticed, then that's what you have to do . . . It's nothing compared with what I've done . . . What did you do in the war, Mummy? Well, I wasn't in the Resistance. I'll tell you that for nothing.

I thought men grew on trees. I really did. There's never been a time in my life when I couldn't pluck someone off at will. Never. Till now. Till just recently . . . ah, sod the lot of them. They're not worth it.

(*Pause.*)

You know when people hang themselves, what do they do first? Do they put the rope around their neck, or do they attach it to the hook, or whatever, that's going to take their weight? And then put it around? They've got to secure it to something as well, haven't they? . . . They must put it round their neck last—next to last—because otherwise they'd have too much. They'd just stand there looking foolish.

(*Pause.*)

I watched a peasant woman skin a rabbit once. It was hanging upside down in her farmyard. She scooped its eyes out first. Kind of scraped them out with a knife. Then she skinned it. Very clean. Not a drop of blood. A kind of quiet dignity. A skilful art. It's amazing how small a rabbit's head looks with its fur off and no ears. It was a fascinating performance. It was dextrous, and solemn. Almost hypnotic. Of course, she must've got it in the jugular first.

I think it's better if you don't remember it, that blow. That one that really hurts. Just get over it quick and go on to something else. Another town. Another audience . . . What d'ye think they give you anaesthetics for in hospital? If they wanted you to enjoy pain, they'd never put you to sleep. You come out of your operation and it's gone, whatever it was that was bothering you. They've cut it out. It's in the bin. They'll burn it for you. You don't even have to do it yourself. They'll take it away and you'll forget about it. Nothing'll ever be that bad again. The worst they can do to you is over. You can't lose three legs. You can't . . . Not unless you're Manx.

(*Pause.*)

There was a man once called Raymond. That's not much of a name. This man used to tell me things and quite honestly, although I don't like to admit it, I believed him. I bloody well believed him. This man told me things that I wanted to hear. I used to think about this man while I was doing other, and as it turned out, more useful things. Like blowing my nose. I thought about Raymond for a whole afternoon once while I grouted some tiles in the bathroom. These were tiles behind the bath that reached up to the ceiling. I could've paid someone to do them, but I was feeling creative and it allowed me to indulge my mind with dreams of him. I was not a young woman at the time. I can never look at bathroom fitments now without thinking of him. He's wash-basins, he's plugs, he's bidets. He's wormed his way into every item of sanitary ware that I can conceive of. I see him in bathcubes and

57

tooth mugs and loofahs. He hangs over my towel rail and dangles on a chain between my taps. When I pull back the curtain of my shower I will find him there, waiting, lurking, ready to surprise me. About to pounce. To deal me a death blow.

If I let him. If I don't deal him one first. Of course, in reality, I can't deal him one now because . . . well, because . . .

There was always something strange about Raymond. He smiled involuntarily. He had a nervous tic. It endeared him to me. He wasn't all there. I mean he had doubts . . . I've been doing this for thirty-five years . . .

I think the whole of existence is an accessory. There's something else that we all clip on to. But try as I might I can't figure out what it is. Or where it is. Or who's got it. Or what they're doing with it. Or why . . . I never could.

(*Pause.* JILL *looks around the stage, confused. As an elderly person might.*)

I don't know where to go. I want to get off the stage now, Maurice. I want to go home. Can you show me the way, please? . . . Maurice . . .

(JILL *remembers where she is but is still not in full control.*)

I'm sorry, ladies and gentlemen . . . this isn't typical . . . it's not normal . . . I can always ad lib. I've never forgotten my lines before. I've always had a joke ready. Anyone'll tell you that.

Oh God. My father used to tell a joke about the docks. It was the new bloke on the docks asking the foreman where the urinal was. 'I don't know,' he said. 'How many funnels has she got?'

You need to understand that that joke's years old because they don't have funnels any more. Not like they used to. And the docks are closing down. But it was a good joke once, wasn't it? You can appreciate that, even

58

now . . . it was a good joke for a man with no legs. If he'd lost anything else he might've been wittier. I don't know . . . you never know.

Oh God. He took out his knife and cut up a back street . . . We used to have one but the wheel fell off . . . A woman went into a shop and asked the feller, 'Do you have asparagus tips?' 'No, we don't,' he said, 'Only Woodbines and Embassy Regal' . . . 'May I join you?' a man asked me one time. 'Why?' I said. 'Am I coming apart?' . . . Halitosis is better than no breath at all . . . Just because you're paranoid, it doesn't mean everyone isn't out to get you . . . Some people still understand all this. God be with the days when the boys went in one door and the girls went in the other.

I was brought up by people years older than me. My roots are in the nineteenth century.

Oh God . . . I want a song, Maurice. You've been a wonderful audience, audience. You really have. I won't forget you . . . and I had nothing else planned for tonight. Did you? . . .

Come on, Maurice. All comedians finish on a song. They should finish on a joke, but they don't. That's why they're comedians. They've got things arseways. They're in the wrong setting . . . Oh God.

(*Pause.* MAURICE *starts the music to get* JILL *off.* JILL *sings, but shakily at first:*)*

Though plans may often go wrong
Let 'em hear your voice.
You'll find that rhythm and song
Make the world rejoice.
Make life go with a swing.

---

*'Count Your Blessings and Smile' is published by Campbell Connelly and Co. Ltd.

Laugh at trouble and sing.
Tra la la la la la la lal
Count your blessings and smile.

While you're playing your part
Keep a song in your heart
Tra la la la la la la lal
Count your blessings and smile.

Sing low, sing high
Isn't it grand, beating the band?
Who wants to die?
Oh what a happy land, hie!
Show them what you can do
Make a hullabaloo
Tra la la la la la la lal
Count your blessings and smile.

You've got to get together, swing it around.
Get together swing it around.

Make life go with a swing and a smile
Laugh at trouble and sing all the while
Now count your blessings and smile.
While you're playing your own little part
You've got to keep a song in your heart
Now count your blessings and smile.

(JILL *has difficulty here.*)

Sing low, sing high
Isn't it grand, beating the band?
Who wants to die?
Oh what a happy land, hie!
Show them what you can do
Make a hullabaloo
Hoo hoo hoo hoo ha ha ha ha

60

Count your blessings one two three
Count your blessings four five six
Count your blessings and smile.

(JILL *speaks.*)

Goodnight, ladies and gentlemen. Goodnight.

(JILL *bows and makes a theatrical exit but with a lack of confidence remaining.*)

THE END